The First Rule of Little Brothers

by Jill Davis   illustrated by Sarah McMenemy

Alfred A. Knopf ᔇ New York

W hen I get really mad at my little brother, my dad always says:
"You know the first rule of little brothers, don't you?"

"No," I say. "What is it?"
"Can't you guess?" he says.

All I know is . . . when my
little brother was a baby,

he watched me all the time—
staring and smiling.

Then one day he began to move! Creeping and crawling closer and closer, coming toward me.

First he touched, next he grabbed—*all my stuff!*

"Look how cute he is!" Grandma always said.
"Look how smart he is!" Grandpa always said.

"How about letting your little brother have a turn?" Mom always said.

"No!" I always said.

Then he started to walk.
And he was everywhere!

One day I built the Empire State Building
with blocks. It was huge! Taller than me!

Then
Bro-zilla
walked
into
the
room.

CRASH!

Then he started to talk!
Guess what his favorite words were?

I'd say:
   "I'm going on the slide."
He'd say:

"Me too!"

I'd say:
   "I'm going first."
He'd say:

"Me too!"

I'd say:
    "I am going to the bathroom BY MYSELF!"
And he'd say:
    "Me too!"

AGHHHH!

Of course, there *were* still some things my little brother *couldn't* do.
Like making dinosaurs.

But when I told him he was too little, he didn't believe me.

Then one day we were having ice cream
with our grandpa. And I heard a little
voice say: "Want me to hold the ball
while you eat your ice cream?"
And I said: "Thanks."

Then my little brother went to his first day of school.
And when he came home, he told me:
"I played superheroes on the rooftop. I made in the potty.
I built the Empire State Building."
Wow. He did all that?

On his second day of school, my little brother brought home a new friend. First they built the Empire State Building.

Next they made a life-size castle.

Then they began playing marbles!

"Hey, guys?" I asked. "Um, can I play, too?"
"Yep," said my little brother. "You can play the winner. Me!"

Now I know the first rule of little brothers:
ALWAYS DO WHAT YOUR BIG BROTHER IS DOING.

But I think I figured out the first rule for us big brothers, too:
ALWAYS BE NICE TO YOUR LITTLE BROTHER, EVEN IF HE
DRIVES YOU CRAZY. Because...

. . . SOMEDAY YOUR LITTLE BROTHER IS GOING TO BE . . .

JUST LIKE YOU!

THIS IS A BORZOI BOOK PUBLISHED BY ALFRED A. KNOPF

Text copyright © 2008 by Jill Davis
Illustrations copyright © 2008 by Sarah McMenemy

Visit us on the Web! www.randomhouse.com/kids

Educators and librarians, for a variety of teaching tools, visit us at www.randomhouse.com/teachers

Library of Congress Cataloging-in-Publication Data
Davis, Jill.
The first rule of little brothers / by Jill Davis ; [illustrations by Sarah McMenemy]. — 1st ed.
p. cm.
Summary: A young boy learns that while his little brother's constant mimicking may be annoying,
it is also a sign of admiration.
ISBN 978-0-375-84046-3 (trade) — ISBN 978-0-375-94046-0 (lib. bdg.)
[1. Brothers—Fiction.] I. McMenemy, Sarah, ill. II. Title.
PZ7.D2885Fi 2008
[E]—dc22
2007044314

The illustrations in this book were created using mixed media.

MANUFACTURED IN CHINA
November 2008
10 9 8 7 6 5 4 3 2 1

First Edition

For Henry, the best little brother ever.
For Gus, the best big brother ever.
But most of all for their dad, Eric, who taught us the rule.
—J.D.

For my brothers, Alex and Tom
—S.M.